My Little Cabin
by Alice Palace

bearpaw books

My name is Marvin
and my little cabin
is way up North,
deep in the woods
where the pine trees grow.

I look out my window
late at night,
wishing I could fly
when I shut
my eyes tight!

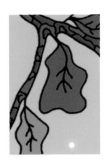

Let's see, Let's see, What can I be?

We're proud majestic eagles
soaring high above the trees,
diving through the clouds
landing on a nest of leaves.

We feed our little eaglets
and guide them as they grow.
They raise their eyes toward the sky,
flap their wings, and begin to fly.

Let's see, Let's see, What else can I be?

We're slippery little fish
bobbin' up and down,
swirling and twirling
our bubbles are all around.

When we're done playing and it's time to go,
we flip our tails, wave our fins
splishing and splashing,
we're ready to swim.

Let's see, Let's see, What else can I be?

Who-Whoo!
We're wise old owls
hooting high up in the trees,
flying all around
then hiding in the leaves.

Our big yellow eyes
watch everything below,
don't you ever wonder
what do we know?

Let's see, Let's see, What else can I be?

We're little green turtles
crawling so slow,
taking our time
wherever we go.

We stretch out our necks
and look all around,
then pop our heads in
without making a sound.

Let's see, Let's see,
What else can I be?

We're noisy little woodpeckers
tapping on a tree,
hopping up and down
as busy as can be.

We climb inside the hollow
to take a little rest,
when our nap is over
we hop out of the nest.

Let's see, Let's see, What else can I be?

We're magnificent moose
ambling and rambling,
running wild and loose.

We wear antlers on top
like a crown,
rubbing and scraping them
up and down, all around.

Let's see, Let's see, What else can I be?

Hippity-hop!
We're slippery spotted frogs
swimming and jumping
on small green pods.

Hopping and skipping
from one petal to the next,
we catch tasty treats
which one is best?

Let's see, Let's see, What else can I be?

We're prickly,
stickily porcupines
sitting on a branch so high.

We munch and crunch twigs and leaves
keeping watch up in the trees.
Crawling down after dark,
we're armed with quills
so long and sharp.

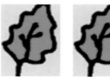

Let's see, Let's see, What else can I be?

We're chubby little cubs
sleeping under a snow covered cap,
in a hollow by a tree
for a long winter's nap.

All curled up
in our dark secret den,
we cuddle and snuggle
till spring comes again.

Let's see, Let's see, What else can I be?

We're sleek shiny beavers
chewing on a tree,
swimming back and forth
as fast as we can be.

We drag all our branches
into the den,
then swim back out
starting over again.

Let's see, Let's see, What else can I be?

We're sleepy baby loons
paddling quietly along.
Mama Loon is calling
crooning her special song.

Cradling us gently
she keeps us warm and fed,
then we fall fast asleep
on her soft feather bed.

Let's see, Let's see,
What else can I be?

We're spotted little fawns
hobbling and wobbling along,
exploring our forest
from dusk until dawn.

Stopping to rest
in a meadow of grass,

we fall fast asleep…

Sweet dreams at last!

Technical Assistance by Carrie Smeby
Illustrations Colorized by Stephen Spencer
Graphic Design by Beth E. Koch

ISBN 0-9709444-0-3
LCCN TXu 944-139

For more information contact:
bearpaw books
P.O. Box 243
Emily, MN 56447
http://www.bearpawbooks.com/

Printed in the United States of America